# THE Matzo Ball Boy

*by* Lisa Shulman

*illustrations by*
Rosanne Litzinger

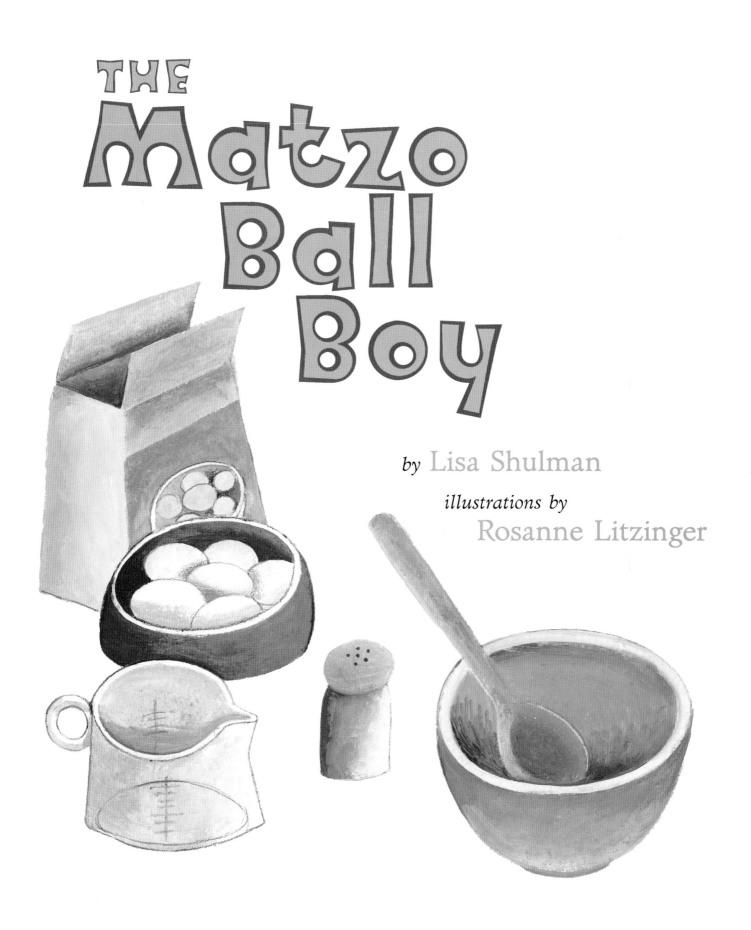

Dutton Children's Books • *New York*

Once upon a time there was an old grandmother, a *bubbe*, who lived all alone. She lived in a tiny cottage at the edge of a small village in a far-off country whose name sounded like a sneeze. Her children were grown with children of their own, but could they be bothered to visit their mother? Not that she was complaining, but she couldn't help feeling lonely.

Soon Passover would be here, and there was no one to come to her *seder*, the holiday dinner. No one to help retell the Passover story. No one to eat her sweet apple-and-walnut *haroset* and sip her delicious matzo ball soup.

So the morning of Passover, the *bubbe* decided to make herself a matzo ball boy. A friendly face in her soup was better than nothing, she thought.

She mixed matzo meal with eggs, oil, salt, and water. From the dough she shaped a soft little body and a round matzo ball head. She gave him a carrot-slice nose, a curving celery mouth, and peppercorn eyes and buttons. Then she plopped him into a pot of chicken soup to cook.

Soon the most delicious smells wafted from the bubbling pot. When the old woman lifted the lid to see if the matzo ball boy was done, out he jumped.

"*Oy!*" she cried in surprise. "And where do you think you're going, my little matzo ball boy?"

The matzo ball boy puffed out his soft little chest. "Boy-shmoy. I'm the matzo ball man, *bubbe*, and I'm off to see the world." Then he ran out the door, leaving smears of *schmaltz*, or chicken fat, on her freshly mopped kitchen floor. Not that she minded a little work, but would it have hurt him to wipe his feet?

"Wait! Wait!" the old woman cried, running after him. "Put on a jacket or you'll catch your death of cold!"

But the matzo ball boy just laughed and kept on running. He called back over his shoulder:

> **"Run, run, as fast as you can.
> You can't catch me.
> I'm the matzo ball man!"**

The old *bubbe* ran as fast as she could, but she couldn't catch him.

The matzo ball boy ran on and on through the village. As he passed the tailor shop, the *schneider* put the last stitch in the rabbi's good coat, which he was patching for Passover, then rubbed his stomach. "*Oy! Oy!* You look good enough to eat, little matzo ball boy!"

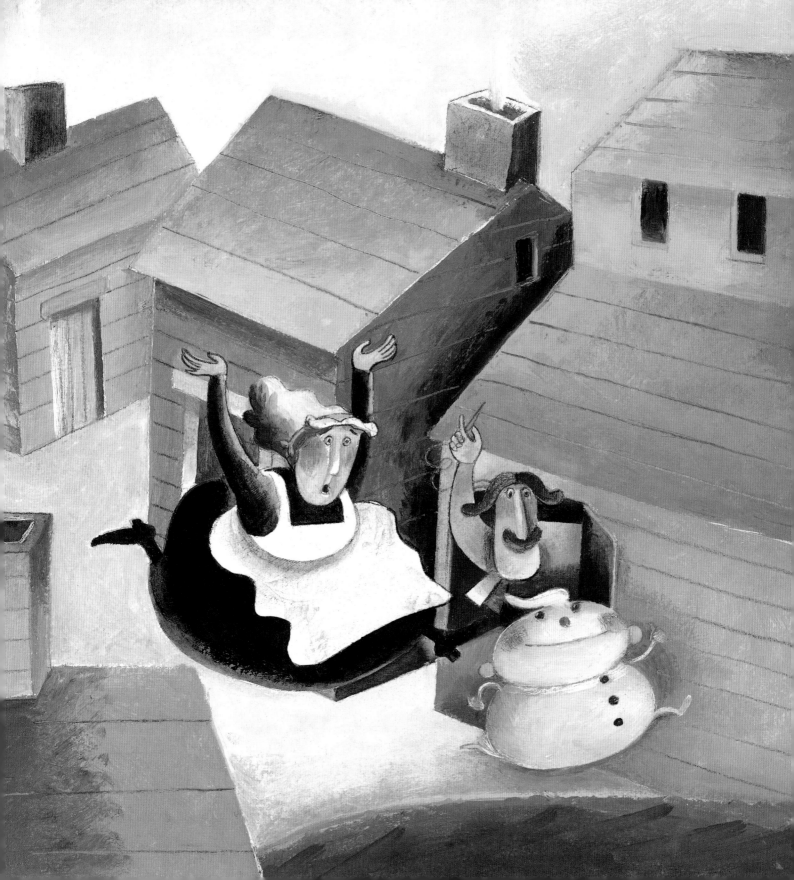

But the matzo ball boy just laughed and kept on running. He called back over his shoulder: "I've run away from my *bubbe*, and I can run away from you, too!"

"So run, run, as fast as you can.
You can't catch me.
I'm the matzo ball man!"

The *schneider* and the old *bubbe* ran as fast as they could, but they couldn't catch him.

The matzo ball boy ran on and on. Soon he passed the *yenta*, the village gossip, and her ten children coming home from the market with apples, nuts, and bitter herbs for their *seder*. The *yenta* dropped her basket and cried, "*Oy! Oy!* You look good enough to eat, little matzo ball boy!"

But the matzo ball boy just laughed and kept on running. He called back over his shoulder: "I've run away from my *bubbe* and the *schneider*, and I can run away from you, too!"

And then, just to show off, he repeated, "Run, run, as fast as you can...." eleven times—once for each of the children and once more for the *yenta* herself.

The *yenta*, her children, the *schneider*, and the old *bubbe* ran as fast as they could, but they couldn't catch that matzo ball boy.

Then the matzo ball boy ran faster than ever. It wasn't long before he came to the rabbi on his way to synagogue. The rabbi licked his lips and said, "*Oy! Oy!* You look good enough to eat, little matzo ball boy!"

But the matzo ball boy just laughed and kept on running. He called back over his shoulder: "I've run away from my *bubbe*, the *schneider*, the *yenta* and her children, and I can run away from you, too!"

"So run, run, as fast as you can.
You can't catch me.
I'm the matzo ball man!"

The rabbi, the *yenta* and her children, the *schneider*, and the old *bubbe* ran as fast as they could, but they couldn't catch him.

The matzo ball boy ran on and on until he came to the edge of a wide river. He could hear the others behind him getting closer and closer.

"*Oy vey!* So now I have to cross a river, too?" The matzo ball boy slapped his forehead. "I'll never see the world at this rate!"

"If you'd care to climb on my back, I'll take you across," said a voice as smooth as *schmaltz*.

The matzo ball boy turned to find a hungry fox grinning at him. "Ha! You must think I'm a real *schlemiel*!" said the matzo ball boy. "Do you think I don't know that old trick? First you get me on your back, then on your head, then onto your nose, and then I'm nothing more than a *nosh* for you! *Feh!*"

The fox smiled a toothy grin. "I can hear the others even closer now. Do you plan to wait here for them?"

"Not on your life, *boychik!*" The matzo ball boy laughed. "For someone who came from a pot of hot soup, this river will be a refreshing change. I'm not made of gingerbread, you know. Me, I'm going for a swim!" And with that, the matzo ball boy jumped into the river and began swimming across.

The fox jumped in, too, but after only a few strokes, he saw he would never catch up with the quick little matzo ball boy. He turned back, grumbling about cold food.

When the matzo ball boy reached the far shore, he looked back and saw the dripping fox, the rabbi, the *yenta* and her children, the *schneider*, and the old *bubbe* standing on the other side calling, "*Oy! Oy!* Come back, come back, little matzo ball boy!"

But the matzo ball boy just laughed and called:

> "Swim, swim, as fast as you can.
> You can't catch me.
> I'm the matzo ball man!"

And since none of the others could swim, except for the fox who pretended he no longer cared, they turned away and began the long walk back to town.

The old *bubbe* was the last to leave.

"So go, go! Have a good time!" she called. "Not that I'm complaining, but is this the thanks I get for bringing you up from a bit of dough?"

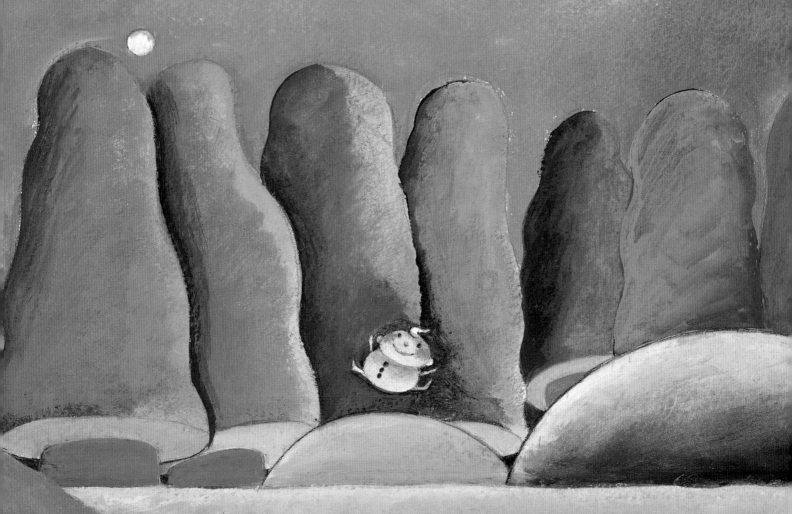

The matzo ball boy watched them go and then, having nothing better to do, set off through the forest that lined the river's edge.

It began to grow dark and cold, and soon the hungry and tired matzo ball boy felt he could walk no farther.

Just then, he came upon a poor man dressed in rags. The matzo ball boy was about to run away when the man said kindly, "*Oy! Oy! You need something good to eat, little matzo ball boy!*"

The matzo ball boy nodded tiredly. "I've run away from my *bubbe*, the *schneider*, the *yenta* and her children, the rabbi, and a fox, and I could run away from you, too, if I wanted. Of course, I wouldn't refuse an offer of a good meal and a soft bed." The matzo ball boy looked expectantly at the man.

"No one should be alone and hungry on Passover," said the man.
"Come home with me. Our food is simple and our cottage small, but
you are welcome to join our meal."

So the matzo ball boy followed the poor man through the forest
until they came to a tiny cottage, hardly bigger than a shack.

Candlelight glowed warmly from the windows, and a fire crackled cheerily in the grate. The man's wife sat by the fire, stirring a big pot of soup. The most delicious smell wafted from the pot, reminding the matzo ball boy of something, though he couldn't think what.

"Welcome!" said the woman with a smile.

"Come in, come in!" said the man. The matzo ball boy took a step inside. "Don't just stand there by the door, where it's cold," said the man. "Come nearer to the fire and warm yourself." He held his hands out to the dancing flames and sighed in contentment.

The matzo ball boy drew closer to the fire. Its heat made him feel relaxed and drowsy.

"The soup will be ready soon," said the woman. She tasted a spoonful, then shook her head in disappointment. "It seems a bit thin tonight. I can't tell what else it needs, can you?"

She held out the spoon to the matzo ball boy, who took it, and leaned over the pot to scoop up a taste. And then...

Well, who's to say how it happened? Perhaps he fell in...perhaps he was pushed? All we know is that the poor man and his hungry wife had a delicious meal of matzo ball soup that night.

(You were maybe expecting a different ending?)

# Author's Note

Passover (also known as *Pesach*) is a Jewish holiday that occurs in the spring. It is a time when Jewish people celebrate the Israelites' escape from Egyptian slavery more than 3,000 years ago. An important part of this celebration is the Passover *seder*, a dinner at which the story of how the Jews became a free people is retold. Special foods are eaten to remember both the bitterness of slavery and the sweetness of freedom.

At Passover, Jews eat a flat, crackerlike bread called *matzo*, as well as delicious dumplings called *matzo balls*, made from the same flour. Traditionally, matzo balls remain in the soup and don't go running off to see the world, but who's to say it couldn't happen?

# Glossary
(The capitalized syllable is stressed in pronunciation.)

*boychik* (BOY-chik) • a tricky fellow; boy
*bubbe* (BUB-beh) • grandmother
*feh* • phooey
*haroset* (ha-ROH-set) • a mixture of chopped apples and nuts
*matzo* (MOTT-seh) • unleavened bread
*matzo ball* • a kind of dumpling made from matzo meal
*nosh* • a little bite to eat; a snack
*oy* • oh!
*oy vey* • oh dear!
*schlemiel* (shleh-MEAL) • a fool
*schmaltz* (SHMALTZ) • chicken fat
*schneider* (SHNY-der) • a tailor
*seder* (SAY-der) • the ritual Passover meal
*yenta* (YEN-ta) • a gossip

For my grandmothers, Rose and Ruth

L.S.


For Donna, David, and Max, with love

R.L.


•

Text copyright © 2005 by Lisa Shulman
Illustrations copyright © 2005 by Rosanne Litzinger

*Library of Congress Cataloging-in-Publication Data*

Shulman, Lisa.
The matzo ball boy/by Lisa Shulman; illustrated by Rosanne Litzinger.—1st ed.
p. cm.
Summary: In this Jewish version of "The Gingerbread Boy," a matzo ball runs away from
an old woman as she prepares her Passover dinner.
ISBN 0-525-47169-3
[1. Passover—Fiction. 2. Jews—Fiction. 3. Fairy tales.] I. Litzinger, Rosanne, ill. II. Title.
PZ8.S345156Mat 2005
[E]—dc22   2004010825

Published in the United States 2005 by Dutton Children's Books,
a division of Penguin Young Readers Group
345 Hudson Street, New York, New York 10014
www.penguin.com

Manufactured in China
First Edition
1 3 5 7 9 10 8 6 4 2